THE ARABIAN NIGHTS
CHILDREN'S COLLECTION

Dados Internacionais de Catalogação na Publicação (CIP) de acordo com ISBD

J76m   Jones, Kellie
          The merchant and the genie / adaptado por Kellie Jones. – Jandira : W. Books, 2025.
          96 p. ; 12,8cm x 19,8cm. – (The Arabian nights)

          ISBN: 978-65-5294-178-7

          1. Literatura infantojuvenil. 2. Contos. 3. Contos de Fadas. 4. Literatura Infantil.
          5. Clássicos. 6. Mágica. 7. Histórias. I. Título. II. Série.

2025-599   CDD 028.5
                                                                                                     CDU 82-93

Elaborado por Vagner Rodolfo da Silva - CRB-8/9410
Índice para catálogo sistemático:
1. Literatura infantojuvenil 028.5
2. Literatura infantojuvenil 82-93

The Arabian Nights 10 Book Collection
Text © Sweet Cherry Publishing Limited, 2023
Inside illustrations © Sweet Cherry Publishing Limited, 2023
Cover illustrations © Sweet Cherry Publishing Limited, 2023

Text based on translations of the original folk tale,
adapted by Kellie Jones
Illustrations by Ella Hood

© 2025 edition:
Ciranda Cultural Editora e Distribuidora Ltda.

1st edition in 2025
www.cirandacultural.com.br
No part of this publication may be reproduced, stored in a retrieval
system, or transmitted in any form or by any means, electronic,
mechanical, photocopying, recording, or otherwise, without written
permission of the publisher.
This book is a work of fiction. Names, characters, places, and incidents
are either the product of the author's imagination or are used fictitiously,
and any resemblance to actual persons, living or dead, business
establishments, events, or locales is entirely coincidental.

The Merchant and the Genie

W. Books

Long ago, in the ancient lands of Arabia, there lived a brave woman called Scheherazade. When the country's sultan went mad, Scheherazade used her cleverness and creativity to save many lives – including her own. She did this over a thousand and one nights, by telling the sultan stories of adventure, danger and enchantment.

These are just some of them …

Shahrayar
The sultan

The Vizier
*Shahrayar's advisor/
Scheherazade's father*

Scheherazade
The new sultana

The Genie
An angry genie

The Merchant
A wealthy trader

The First Man
A man with a deer

The Second Man
A man with two dogs

The Third Man
A man with a donkey

Prologue

There once was a sultan whose name was Shahrayar.

Shahrayar had a wife whom he loved more than anything. He showered her with gifts, from the finest dresses to the most beautiful jewels – though none of them were as beautiful as her, he insisted.

He was generous with his time, too, spending as much of it with

> **sultan**
> *A type of ruler or king in Islamic countries.*

his wife as he could. But he was still a ruler, and rulers are often busy, especially if they are good ones.

Shahrayar was a very good ruler. At least in the beginning ...

Then there came a time when his wife stopped sighing over new dresses, and she refused to wear her new jewels. Her eyes no longer lit up when her husband went to her. Shahrayar puzzled over this, until one day his wife ran away with another man.

As great as Shahrayar's love had been before, his heartbreak was just as great now. His pain knew no limit, his rage no end. He was convinced that wives could not be trusted, and he vowed never to marry again.

'But you *must* marry,' said his advisors. 'You must marry and have a family, otherwise there will be no one to rule the kingdom after you die. Your enemies will see it as a weakness. They will attack.'

'Then if I do marry, I will not love her. In fact, I will have any wife executed before I ever allow myself to feel this pain again.'

---

executed
Historically, when someone was killed as punishment by law.

This was a wicked promise indeed, and word of it soon spread. The people's love for the sultan turned to fear, and no father wanted their daughter to become the next sultana.

One of these fathers was Shahrayar's vizier. It was the vizier's job to find a new bride, and he refused to do it. How could he sentence an innocent woman to death? Especially when he had two daughters of his own. But as time

sultana
The wife, unmarried partner or close female relative of a sultan.

vizier
A high-ranking advisor to the royal family in the old Turkish empire and in Islamic countries.

passed, and enemies gathered, it became more and more important that the sultan remarry.

'Father,' said the vizier's eldest daughter one day, 'I have a favour to ask of you. One I am afraid you will not like.'

'What is it, Scheherazade?' he asked wearily, for war was looming and the sultan had clearly gone mad.

'Let me marry Shahrayar,' said Scheherazade.

The vizier could only stare at her. Scheherazade was clever. He had educated her and her sister himself. They had learnt philosophy, medicine, history and fine arts, and Scheherazade excelled at all of them. She was brave and beautiful, too, but what she

had just said was madness – and he told her so.

'Trust me, father, I have a plan. I will not let any woman die just because the sultan needs a wife and fears falling in love with her.'

'So *you* will die instead?' her father demanded. 'He could have you executed the morning after the wedding if he chose! And do not forget the story of the donkey, the ox and the merchant.'

'What story is that?'

So her father told her.

merchant
Someone who buys and sells goods.

Chapter 1

The Story of the Donkey, the Ox and the Merchant

This is the story of a merchant who could understand animals. No one knew he could do this, least of all the animals, but he liked to visit the barn sometimes and listen.

One day he heard his ox complaining to his donkey, 'You are so lucky! I wish I were as well cared for as you. You are given fresh, clean water and fine, sifted barley. You only have to carry the master from time to time, while I have to pull the plough every day through every field. The yoke hurts my neck and yet I am whipped to make me work faster.

At night I return to nothing but bad beans and chaff in my trough.'

The donkey, lying comfortably in his stall, replied, 'If you were as brave as you are strong, they would not dare to treat you so badly. Why do you not fight back? Your horns, your hooves and your bellows would terrify them. Refuse to eat the bad beans and they will have to bring you something better.'

'Do you really think so?' asked the ox.

'I do,' replied the donkey.

The merchant, listening in, said nothing.

Early the next morning, the herdsman came for the ox. He took him to the plough as usual, but the ox was not his usual obedient self. He bellowed and tossed his head so much that the herdsman could not get the yoke on his neck. When the herdsman tried to tie the ox to his stall,

herdsman
Someone similar to a shepherd or a farmer who looks after and moves animals around for a living.

the ox kicked and charged with his horns until the herdsman was afraid to go near him. Finally, the ox refused to eat the beans in his trough.

In short, he did exactly as the donkey had advised.

'Well done!' the donkey congratulated him.

'Thank you,' said the ox, 'but I am almost as tired from fighting as I was from working!'

'Then tomorrow do not do anything at all,' advised the donkey. 'Just lie there. They cannot make you move – you are too big.'

When the herdsman came again the next morning, he found the ox's trough still full of food and the ox lying on the ground. The herdsman decided the ox was too ill to work and went to tell the merchant.

The merchant had been waiting for this, and his reply was simple, 'Let the donkey do the work instead.'

So the donkey was yoked to the plough, and his neck hurt even more than the ox's because he was

not used to it, and the work was so slow that he was whipped more, too. When he returned to his stall, he saw his neighbour the ox lying comfortably, chewing fine, sifted barley.

'You were right!' said the ox. 'They cannot make me move. I am never going to work again!'

The donkey was so tired that he dropped down dead.

Scheherazade's father finished his story and smiled affectionately at her. 'You, my child, are just like that donkey: you will bring destruction on yourself by trying to save others from it.'

'And like a donkey, father, I am too stubborn to change my mind. Please present me to the sultan as his bride, or I will present myself.'

The vizier sighed sadly and went to tell Shahrayar that he had found the next sultana, and that she was none other than his own daughter.

Shahrayar was astonished. 'Is it possible,' he said, 'that you can give up your own child?'

'Scheherazade has her own mind, Sire, and she has chosen this path. I cannot steer her off course.'

'She volunteered to marry me?' To Shahrayar, this seemed like further proof that women were untrustworthy. He spoke in a harder tone when he addressed the vizier again.

'Very well, bring her to me. Only do not doubt that the next time you see her may be when you take her to die. If you disobey me when that time comes, you will die too.'

'I will not disobey you,' said the vizier. 'Although I am a father, I am also your subject.' With a bow, he left Shahrayar and went to tell his daughter, 'It is done.'

Scheherazade wiped the tears from his face. 'Thank you, father. In time these will be tears of joy, I promise.'

Before Scheherazade went to the palace, she called for her sister. She told Dinarzade where she was going and why.

'No!' Dinarzade gasped. 'You cannot.'

'I must,' said Scheherazade. 'But I need your help. As soon as I am presented to the sultan, I will ask him to let you stay with us in our room. Then you must promise to wake me at dawn. This is what you must say when you do: "Since it may be the last time, sister, I beg of you, please tell me one of your wonderful stories".'

Dinarzade promised to do this and Scheherazade was escorted to the palace by her father, and into the presence of the sultan. There, for the first time, Scheherazade felt a twinge of fear and doubt.

The room was vast
and growing dim with
nightfall. Above her
head, lanterns of
pierced brass and
glass mosaic hung like
pendulums from the ceiling.
They cast light in all shapes
and colours across the tiled
walls and pale, thin pillars.

The sultan sat on a raised
throne of silk cushions, against
a backdrop of cutwork panels.
The sun was setting behind
him, making his shadowed face
impossible to see.

'Leave us,' he commanded the vizier.

The look Scheherazade's father gave her as he left almost broke her heart. Then she was alone with the sultan.

'Remove your veil,' he ordered.

Scheherazade did. She knew that people thought she was beautiful, but she could not tell if Shahrayar agreed. All he said was, 'You are crying.'

Scheherezade blinked, surprised to find that it was true. *I can use this*, she thought.

'Sire,' she said, 'forgive me. I am only thinking of my dear sister. I would be so grateful if you could allow her to stay with me. It would bring me much comfort.'

Shahrayar agreed to this, for he did indeed think that Scheherazade was very beautiful. So beautiful, in fact, that he sent word to the vizier that he must take her away before breakfast the next morning. Any later and Shahrayar might start to fall in love.

They were married that day, and that night Dinarzade was brought to the palace to stay with her sister. She knew from their father that Scheherazade was to die in the morning. Scheherazade was not surprised to hear it, although she trembled with fear.

'That is why you must do as I asked,' she reminded her sister.

So Dinarzade slept on a velvet couch at the foot of the royal bed. At dawn, she shook her sister awake.

'Scheherezade,' she said, speaking loudly enough to also wake the sultan. 'Since it may be the last time, I beg of you, please tell me one of your wonderful stories.'

Scheherezade turned to her new husband. 'Will Your Majesty permit me to do as my sister asks?'

'Gladly,' he replied.

'Then I will tell you the story of the merchant and the genie ...'

Chapter 2

The Story of the Merchant and the Genie

There was once a wealthy merchant whose business often took him travelling. One day he was riding home from a far-off land when he stopped by a water spring to drink. Afterwards he rested in the shade of a tree, eating bread and dates. When he finished each date, he threw the stone over his shoulder. Before he

had thrown the last one, a genie appeared.

The genie was huge, as was his scimitar – but his rage was greatest of all.

'You killed my son!' he roared.

The merchant denied doing any such thing.

scimitar
A sword with a curved blade that was used in the Middle East.

'Have you been eating dates?' the genie demanded.

'Yes.'

'Did you throw away their stones?'

'Of course.'

'Then you threw the stone that killed my son! Now I will kill *you*.'

With that, the genie advanced with his sword. The curved blade glinted wickedly, carving crescent moons out of sunlight.

'Forgive me!' the merchant cried. 'It was an accident!'

But no matter how much he apologised and begged for his life, it was no good: the genie would not show mercy.

'Very well,' the merchant said at last. 'But if I must prepare for death, there is much to be done. Will you give me time to return home and set my affairs in order?'

'You mean give you time to escape?' the genie laughed. 'Never!'

'I swear I will return to face my punishment in the new year.'

Reluctantly, the genie agreed to wait and trust the merchant's

mercy
Showing kindness and forgiveness.

word. The merchant got back on his horse and rode home. Since he had been gone a while, his family was very happy to see him. But they wept when he told them what had happened.

The next day the merchant began to prepare for his death. He settled his debts, gave gifts to his friends and money to the poor. He made sure his wife and children were provided for. In the new year, he said goodbye.

Returning to the spring where he had met the genie, the merchant saw a man leading a deer.

The man asked him, 'What brings you to this place where there are so many genies about? It is dangerous to stop here, you should move on.'

'If only you had been here when

I first passed through!' said the merchant. 'Your warning comes too late to help me.'

Then the merchant explained why he was there and the man was sorry for him – especially when he saw how the merchant's hands were shaking. He was also curious to see what happened when the genie arrived.

'I will stay with you,' the man said.

Grateful that he would not die alone, the merchant gladly accepted the company.

A little later, another man

passed by leading two dogs. He asked what the men were doing in such a dangerous place. As soon as he heard the answer, he too wanted to stay and see what happened. Finally, a third man passed by with a donkey, asked the same question and made the same decision.

When the genie arrived in a storm of sand and fury, he found four men waiting for him – but he only cared about one. He marched straight up to the merchant and demanded, 'Stand and die!'

The merchant was frozen with fear. To his surprise, the man with the deer threw himself at the genie's feet. 'O mighty Genie, stay your sword and hear my story. If you find it more interesting than the story of yourself and the merchant, I beg you to spare him one third of his punishment.'

'Very well,' the genie agreed. 'I am listening.'

'Then I will begin …'

Chapter 3

The Story of the First Man and the Deer

This deer that you see with me is my wife transformed. After many years together, we had no children of our own. I began to worry about who would take over the running of the farm when I died, and who would care for my wife and me in our old age. I had to make a decision.

I adopted the son of a widow who

---

widow
A woman whose husband has died.

had lived on our land for years. From the instant I made him my heir, however, my wife grew to hate both him and his mother. She saw it as a betrayal, and a sign that I did not love her anymore. But really I was only doing what I thought was best.

When my adopted son was fifteen years old, I was forced to

go on a journey. It would mean leaving my home for months and trusting my wife to look after him and his mother. Alas, while I was gone, my wife used magic to transform my son into a bull and his mother into a cow. She gave both to our herdsman to care for.

When I returned and asked after them, my wife told me that the widow was dead and she had not seen my son for weeks. Of course, I tried to find him, but after eight months of searching there was no sign.

Then came the feast of Eid al-Adha. I ordered the herdsman to bring a cow to sacrifice for the celebration. He did, and the creature bellowed pitifully, as if she knew what was about to happen. It made me pause with the knife.

Eid al-Adha
A Muslim festival for thanking Allah and celebrating a happy occasion.

'Go on,' my wife urged. 'She is the fattest and the best. Kill her.'

But the cow continued to cry and in the end the herdsman killed her for me. Although she had looked plump and healthy, we found that she was nothing but skin and bones.

'What a waste,' I said sadly.

'Fetch another!' commanded my wife. 'A bull – you know the one.'

The herdsman brought a fine young bull. He too was lowing and crying pathetically, and I found that I had quite lost my appetite for meat that year. But my wife insisted, 'A grand celebration must have a grand sacrifice. Kill him.'

She pressed the knife into my palm while the bull pushed his head into my chest. His eyes were almost human as they pleaded, 'Do not kill me!'

'I cannot,' I said at last. 'Maybe next year,' I added, when my wife looked furious. She stormed off, and despite my words I gave the bull to the herdsman. I could not imagine slaughtering him in one year or ten.

The next day, the herdsman returned to find me.

'Master,' he said, 'I have something to tell you that I think you will want to hear. You see, it was your wife who brought me the cow you had slaughtered yesterday, and the bull whom you spared. I never knew where they came from, but yesterday I took the bull home as you asked and my daughter saw him.

'My daughter, who knows magic, tells me that the bull is none other than your adopted son, her childhood friend. And the cow is – *was* ...'

'His mother,' I concluded for him. I felt sick at the thought – but I was not yet convinced by the story.

'Bring me your daughter,' I said.

The herdsman's daughter came before me. She was half smiles and half tears over the animal she said was my son. The smiles were because he was alive after all, and the tears were because he had lost his dear mother – to her father's own hand and my orders. Both reactions were enough to convince me of the terrible truth.

'Can my son be returned to his human body?' I asked her.

'Yes,' she said, 'and I can do it. I have only two conditions: one is that when he is human again you give him to me as my husband; the other is that you let me punish the woman who did this.'

'I agree to both conditions,' I answered. 'I only ask that you let my wife live. We were happy once. She became bitter and angry only when we found that we could not have children of our own. In time, you may forgive what she has done. For now, show mercy.'

'Very well. As she spared your son's life, so I will spare hers.'

The herdsman's daughter
fetched the bull and some water,
which she spoke secret words
over and sprinkled on the animal.
Then he was an animal no more,
but a strong young man.

'My son!' I cried joyfully, kissing him. 'This young woman has rescued you. Would you marry her in return?'

My son was more than happy to accept his childhood sweetheart.

Before they were married, the herdsman's daughter turned my wife into a deer. When the time came for me to go travelling again, I chose not to leave her in the care of others and took her with me.

'And here she is,' the first man concluded, showing the deer and patting her affectionately. 'Is that not an interesting story?'

'It is,' agreed the genie, 'and I will spare the merchant one third of his punishment as I promised. Instead of killing him, I will only hurt him - *badly.*' The genie advanced on the merchant again, and this time the second man with the two dogs pleaded with him.

'I too have a story, great Genie,' he claimed. 'Will you offer me the same deal if I tell it? Will you spare the merchant one third of his punishment if you find it interesting?'

'Very well,' replied the genie, 'but only if it is more interesting than the last one.'

With this agreement, the second man began his story …

Chapter 4

The Story of the Second Man and the Two Dogs

These two dogs are my brothers. When our father died, he left us each a thousand coins. We used them to open our own shops and become merchants. Not long after this, my eldest brother, always impatient, decided to take his business abroad where he hoped to make more money. He sold his shop to pay for passage overseas and did not return for a year. When he did, I did not recognise him. All I saw was a ragged beggar come into my shop.

'Hello, friend,' I said politely.
'Hello, brother,' he replied.

I closed my shop and took him home with me. In the year that had passed, I had made 2000 dinars in profit, while my brother had lost everything he had. I gave him half of the money to open another shop.

'But no more get-rich-quick schemes,' I warned him.

Then my middle brother, bored with hard work and routine, decided that he would go travelling too. He sold his business and set out overland

dinar
The form of money used in ancient Arabia. Still used today in some countries.

in a caravan, returning at the end of a year in the same poor state that our elder brother had. Once again, I had 2000 dinars in savings, so I gave him half and he re-opened his shop.

'Stay here, work steadily, and you will prosper,' I assured him.

But as time passed, I noticed how my brothers' memories of their time away became rosier. They no longer spoke of their experiences as failures, but as adventures. Until one day they

---

caravan
A band of people and animals travelling together, often formed for safety when crossing a remote area like a desert.

said that we should all go on an adventure together.

'We can trade as we go,' said the eldest.

'We can see the world,' said the second eldest.

'You did not do so well trading abroad last time,' I reminded them. 'Nor did the world treat you very well if it turned you into a beggar.'

Thus, I refused. But every year, for six years, they said the same thing. Finally, after many tales of one brother's seafaring and the other's wanderings, I agreed.

'We will need to buy supplies and hire a ship,' I said.

That was when I learnt that my brothers had no money – no savings – at all. They had spent everything. Fortunately, I had 6000 dinars. I shared half with my brothers so that we could each buy merchandise to sell. The rest I buried thinking that we would have enough to return to and rebuild our businesses if necessary.

At the first port we sailed to, I sold what I had bought for ten times the price I paid. I used the profit to buy more goods and my success continued at the next port. And the next. Soon, however, we began to spend longer in each port as my brothers became more interested in having fun than doing business. And I began to understand how they always 'lost' whatever money they had.

---

port
A town or city with direct access to water, where ships can load and unload passengers and goods.

One evening I was waiting for them to finish enjoying themselves, when I saw a woman in rags. I approached her with a handful of coins, but she took my hand instead of the money.

'You are a good man,' she said. 'Marry me and I will be a good wife.'

My brothers appeared at that moment, loud and mean.

'What is this?' they laughed. 'Our little brother making friends with beggars!'

They pushed the woman roughly aside and she fell to the ground. My hand still had the coins in it, which my brothers took.

'Our need is greater than hers!'

As they walked away, I helped the woman to stand. Her knee was bloody. How could my brothers be so unkind when they had been beggars once themselves?

'Come on!' they called back impatiently, as if they had been waiting for *me* all evening and not the other way around.

But I did not wait any more, nor did I follow. Instead I tended to the woman's knee. As I did, I got to know her. I learnt about her love for her sister, who lived far away, and how she had always wanted to open a dress shop. I learnt that beneath her rags was a pure heart, and I decided that, yes, perhaps I needed a wife.

By the time we finally set sail, I was married.

My brothers were not pleased.

'Who is she?' they demanded. They did not recognise her now that she was clean and beautifully dressed. 'What about us? You have so much already!'

It was clear to me by then that they had spent most of the money we set out with, while I had only increased mine. Add to that a pretty wife, and my brothers were more jealous of me than ever. It only got worse as I fell in love and became truly happy. It got so bad, in fact, that one night they plotted to throw us overboard.

That was when I learnt that my wife was a genie. The moment they tried to seize us from our bed, she transformed.

'STOP!' she boomed, towering over them until they trembled with terror. 'Is this how you betray a brother who has given you everything? A man so kind he would marry a beggar just because she asked? You do not deserve him. You do not deserve to *live*!'

'Wait!' I stopped her. 'My love, you cannot kill them.'

'Why not? They are not worthy of my kindness any more than yours! I heard them planning to kill you and take your money. They must be punished!'

'Show mercy,' I told her.

'Unkindness is its own punishment; just as kindness is its own reward.'

For my sake she let my brothers live and flew us both to my old home. I dug up the money I had buried and used it to open the dress shop of her dreams. She wrote to her sister to tell her all about it. Then one day a messenger appeared with two dogs and a reply.

My wife read the letter.

'Oh no,' she said.

'What is it?' I asked.

'My sister decided to find and punish your brothers for me. These dogs are them. She says to look for her in ten years when they have learnt their lesson. Then she will transform them back.'

'It had not occurred to me,' said the second man, 'that my wife's sister must also be a genie. So you see, it is now ten years later. I have left my wife in charge of our business and brought my brothers to find her sister so that they can be returned to their human bodies. That is my story. Was it even more interesting than the last one?'

'Yes, it was,' said the genie, entertained despite himself. 'Very interesting indeed. I will not hurt the merchant, but I will lock him up forever as my prisoner.'

'But,' said the third man with the donkey, 'I know an even better story than the two you have heard already.'

'You do?'

'Yes, merciful Genie. If I tell it to you, will you offer me the final third of the merchant's punishment?'

'If it truly *is* better,' said the genie – and he sounded doubtful, 'then yes, I will …'

Chapter 5

The Story of the Third Man and the Donkey

This donkey is my wife, and I have not been a good husband. I found love too easily and was too young to appreciate how rare it is. I was selfish, with foolish ideas about marriage. I left my wife alone for days, then weeks, then months at a time so that I might go travelling.

'Take me with you,' she would say before I left. 'I want to stay by your side.'

'A wife's place is in the home,' I would reply.

Eventually, I stayed long enough to see our first child born. But soon after, I announced that I would be leaving for a whole year.

Then my wife said, 'Do not go. I want you to stay by my side.'

'A man is not a dog,' I told her. 'He needs freedom and adventure.'

I left her bouncing our baby daughter on her hip, never doubting that she would be waiting for me when I returned. And she was – but she was not alone. There was a man in our house. It had never occurred to me until then that she might fall in love with someone else while I was gone.

'Who was that?' I demanded, when I had all but kicked him out of the door.

'No one,' she said, hiding something behind her back.

'Do not lie to me, I am your husband!'

'And I am your *wife*!' she shouted back. 'All I ever asked was that you stay with me and yet you cannot wait to get away. Even now you are not pleased to see me.'

'That is because you have betrayed me with another man!'

'I have not betrayed you! Unlike you, *I* am loyal.'

'You are my wife! You are *supposed* to be loyal.'

'Like I am supposed to work all day, cooking and cleaning and raising our child by myself? Like you are *supposed* to do whatever you want wherever you please for however long you like? No.' She shook her head fiercely. 'What you need is a donkey, not a wife.'

For the first time, she drew her hand from behind her back. In it was a small glass bottle.

'And what I need is ...' She threw the bottle suddenly at my feet. 'A dog!'

Clear liquid splashed up my legs, which immediately doubled from two to four – and they were furry. I had transformed into a dog. But if my wife had thought I would be the kind of dog that was loyal and loving, that came when called and wagged its tail, she was mistaken. I was the kind that barked and barked. For I still had the mind of a man, and I was angry.

When the baby – *how big she had grown!* – began to cry at the noise, my wife put me outside. I scratched at the door and barked some more. Then I became aware of the many smells around me – including one that I somehow recognised belonged to the man who had given my wife the potion.

I followed the scent with my dog

nose until I found him. He had a travelling stall that jangled with hundreds of glass bottles. I barked until he noticed me. Then, when he ignored me, I barked until his customers were too afraid to shop at his stall. Finally, he took one of the bottles, poured it over me, and I was a man again. And I was *still* angry.

'I want whatever potion you gave my wife,' I demanded.

I returned to my house and scratched at the door as if I were still a dog. My wife opened it and gasped to find that I was *not* still a dog.

'You said I needed a donkey, not a wife,' I reminded her. 'So be it.'

With a splash of the potion, she transformed into a donkey. But if I had thought she would be the kind of donkey that did as it was told and waited quietly until then, it was my turn to be mistaken. She was the kind that bit and bit – and, for good measure, *kicked*.

Without my wife, I had to care for

our daughter by myself. That was not so bad, because she was delightful. I enjoyed getting to know her after being away for most of her young life. But I also had to cook and clean and keep house, and that was not delightful. It was hard work!

I am embarrassed to say that by the third day, I went in search of the man with the potions. I wanted to get the antidote and transform my wife back to her human self. More than that,

antidote
A medicine that stops poison from working or cures a disease.

I wanted to apologise for all that I had done to her, now that I could finally appreciate all that she had done for me. But I was too late.

The potion seller was gone.

I left my daughter with my sister and I have been travelling from town to town ever since in search of him, only this time my wife has travelled with me.

The third man stopped talking and stroked the donkey carefully. 'I only hope she will forgive me one day.' Perhaps his wife had heard his plea, for she did not bite him.

The genie sighed. 'Very well. I will not kill the merchant *or* hurt him *or* lock him up. Your three wonderful stories have saved him, and they have taught me something about forgiveness as well.'

With that, the genie vanished.

The merchant thanked the three men who had saved his life, and returned to his family who were shocked and delighted to see him. He never ate dates carelessly again.

The first man's adopted son and daughter-in-law eventually forgave his wife. The second man reached his sister-in-law, who decided that his brothers had indeed learnt their lesson. The third man found the potion seller and decided that he was more than ready to stop travelling and stay home with his wife and daughter.

Epilogue

By the time Scheherazade had finished her story, the sun had risen in the sky. A second later, there was a knock at the door. It was her father coming to take her away. She was about to be executed.

Scheherazade held her breath and felt across the bedclothes for Dinarzade's hand. She squeezed it and felt her sister's answering squeeze back. It gave her courage and steadied her voice when it would have trembled.

'Did you enjoy my story, Your Majesty?'

The sultan felt as if he were waking from a long, wonderful dream – and he was sad that it had ended.

'I enjoyed it very much,' he admitted. 'I have never heard a finer story.'

'Then I am sorry I did not tell you the story of the fisherman and the genie, for that one is better still.'

The second knock at the door made Scheherazade jump.

Shahrayar ignored it.

'Even better than the story of the merchant and the genie?' he asked – and he sounded doubtful.

'Yes,' said Scheherazade, 'much better. If you like,' she added, 'I could tell it to you. Tonight, perhaps?'

It would mean delaying the execution, but the sultan was curious – just as Scheherazade had hoped he would be.

Besides, Shahrayar thought, *it is only for one more night.*

'Very well,' he said at last. 'Tonight you will tell me one

more story.' Then Shahrayar left the room, taking his confused but relieved vizier with him.

'You did it!' cried Dinarzade. 'You survived the morning!'

Scheherazade hugged her sister and walked out onto the balcony to breathe in the new day.

'Just as I will survive tomorrow morning,' she promised. 'And the morning after that. And the morning after that ...'

And so began a thousand and one nights of storytelling ...